MARIA CHAPDELAINE

Based on the novel by LOUIS HÉMON

❖ PAINTINGS BY RAJKA KUPESIC ❖

TUNDRA BOOKS

Originally published in France in serial form in 1914
First published in Canada in book form in 1916
First published by Tundra Books in French and English in 1989
First published in this abridged edition by Tundra Books in 2004

Published in Canada by Tundra Books,
481 University Avenue, Toronto, Ontario M5G 2E9

Published in the United States by Tundra Books of Northern New York,
P.O. Box 1030, Plattsburgh, New York 12901

Library of Congress Control Number: 2004100578

National Library of Canada Cataloguing in Publication

Hémon, Louis, 1880-1913
    Maria Chapdelaine / Louis Hémon ; paintings by Rajka Kupesic.

ISBN 0-88776-697-8

    I. Kupesic, Rajka II. Title.

PQ2615.E35M313 2004   843'.912   C2004-900491-3

We acknowledge the financial support of the Government of Canada through the Book Publishing
Industry Development Program (BPIDP) and that of the Government of Ontario through the Ontario
Media Development Corporation's Ontario Book Initiative. We further acknowledge the support of the
Canada Council for the Arts and the Ontario Arts Council for our publishing program.

The publisher extends sincere appreciation to author Marthe Jocelyn for her graceful
and sensitive abridgement.

Medium: oil on linen

Design: Terri Nimmo

Printed in Hong Kong, China

1 2 3 4 5 6   09 08 07 06 05 04

It has been a long winter of crackling cold in the village of Peribonka. The men and women wear their fur coats against the chill.

But today there is a breath of spring in the air.

"Soon the ice will break up on the river," reports the blacksmith.

Maria Chapdelaine has been away for a month, visiting relatives in Saint-Prime. When she comes to church, the young men admire her from a distance.

"A fine girl!" says one.

"And a hard worker!" says another. "Too bad she lives so deep in the woods. Who wants to drive a horse for twelve miles and cross the river to spend an evening with a girl?"

As Maria and her father pass by, the young men blush and step back. All except one. François Paradis welcomes the rare chance to say hello to Samuel Chapdelaine and his daughter. Maria hasn't seen François for seven years. His eyes are eager and bright.

"I'm working as a guide for some Belgians who want to buy furs from the Indians," he explains. "We'll be camping near your farm in a couple of weeks, once the ice breaks up. I would like to visit one evening."

"Fine, François," says Samuel. "We'll look out for you."

Maria now has another reason to look forward to spring.

The Chapdelaines set out for the long drive home.

Their horse, like every horse ever owned by their family, is named Charles-Eugène. Long ago there was a Chapdelaine who quarreled with his neighbor called Charles-Eugène. He gave the name to his horse so that he could feel triumph whenever he shouted, "You useless slouch of a half-broken-in old donkey! Charles-Eugène! Giddy-up, there!"

The icy road runs beside the snow-covered river. Here and there are houses, sitting on small plots of cleared land, surrounded by the dark, green forest. When the sleigh reaches the crossing point on

the Peribonka River, Charles-Eugène pauses to sniff the ice,
then trots out onto the frozen surface.

But halfway across there is a loud *CRACK*, and the ice beneath
the sleigh runners shifts as water seeps up from below.

"Giddy-up, Charles-Eugène!" cries Samuel Chapdelaine.
"Get on, now!"

The horse gallops to the shore, arriving just as the ice slides away
behind them.

"I guess we're the last to cross this season!" shouts Samuel.

At home, the family is waiting to hear all the news of Maria's month away. Her brother Télesphore is outside feeding the cows, but her little sister, Alma-Rose, and her brother Ti'Bé crowd around while their mother, Laura, puts supper on the table. And Chien, the dog, who missed Maria too, wants a pat.

Maria looks around the cabin, half-wishing something might have changed while she was away. But it is all familiar: the big stove, the tall cupboard, the table and bench, the beds, and the ladder up to the boys' sleeping loft.

Maria's family are not the only ones happy to have her home. Their closest neighbor, Eutrope Gagnon, has trudged through two miles of snowy woods to say hello. Although the talk is about the long winter and how hard it is on the animals, Maria feels Eutrope's eyes watching her.

"And come spring, we'll clear more land," declares Samuel. "When the older boys are back from the logging camps, we'll get to work."

"Spring is not so far," Maria says, wistfully.

One morning Maria opens the door and hears the thunder of the nearby waterfall that has been silent all winter. "The ice is gone!" she exclaims. "Spring is here – and mud!"

Only a few nights later, François Paradis arrives long after dark and is greeted by Chien's barking. "I apologize for coming so late," he says, his blue eyes shining.

But Maria's mother is pleased to have a visitor, whatever the time. "You sold the farm when your father died, François?" she asks.

"Yes," he says. "I would not be happy as a farmer, staying in one place year after year. I like to be in the woods, working as a logger or a trader or a guide. I like to be on the move."

Laura Chapdelaine shakes her head at him in wonder. There are men like her husband, who work hard to settle the land; and there are men like François, who chase adventure in its vast wilds.

When François says good night, he promises to return in a few weeks. Maria blushes, feeling a drumming in her heart.

Finally, in June, the sun begins to warm the earth. The real spring has come. Maria's older brothers, Esdras and Da'Bé, arrive home from the logging camps. With them comes Edwidge Légaré, who will help the Chapdelaines clear land during the summer.

Tree stumps, tangled roots, and fallen logs clutter the ground between the cabin and the deep woods. One by one, every obstacle must be removed to clear a field that will someday be planted with crops. Wielding axes and chains, the men work until the sweat runs into their eyes.

Flies and mosquitoes torment the workers. The sun is ferocious. Maria brings water to the field for the men to guzzle. She and her mother also serve lunch: pea soup, salt pork and boiled potatoes, hot tea and thick slices of bread soaked in maple syrup.

Each time the sun sets, the land is one day closer to being tamed and ploughed.

The blueberries are ripe by early July, ready for the Feast of Saint Anne. The Chapdelaines host a party unlike any their little cabin has ever seen. Eutrope Gagnon is there, and Edwidge Légaré, who tells stories of building the railroad to Québec City thirty years ago.

Chien barks at the sound of footsteps outside. Maria's heart skips a beat. *Is it François Paradis?*

But no, it is Ephrem Surprenant from Honfleur and his nephew, Lorenzo, who works in the United States. Everyone is amazed to hear about life in a splendid American city.

"How big a place is it, where you live?" asks Maria's mother.

"Ninety thousand," says Lorenzo.

"Ninety thousand! Bigger than Québec City," she says.

The open door frames the sunset over the immense forest. But with the evening comes a cloud of mosquitoes. Télesphore fills a pail with dry chips and twigs, and sets it alight. When the flame burns high, he adds grass and leaves, causing a smoke that chases away the insects.

Alma-Rose sings as the smoke clings to the walls:

> *Fly, fly, leave my face,*
> *My nose is not a public place.*

"Good evening!" François exclaims, as he steps through the doorway. Maria's heart jumps. *Here he is, at last.*

Laura Chapdelaine is nearly as happy as her daughter – she has five visitors at the same time! And if she paid attention, she would see that the three young men are all watching Maria with great admiration. As the evening goes by, each one steals as many glances as he dares. Finally, after stories and card games, it is time for the company to leave.

"But you'll stay, won't you, François?" asks Samuel.

"Of course he will," insists Laura. "He can sleep in the loft with the boys."

For Maria, this brings François into the family.

The next morning, François washes and shaves and borrows clean clothes from Da'Bé. Laura Chapdelaine tells him how fine he looks.

The whole family gathers tin cups and bowls and pails for the blueberry-picking expedition. The berries are plump and ripe, purple clusters hanging from the stalks. Maria and François find themselves alone, kneeling amidst the bushes to fill their buckets.

"Maria," says François. "I hope you've heard no bad stories about me."

"No," says Maria.

"I'm going to work hard this winter at a lumber camp and save all my money. I'll be back in the spring. Will you still be here?"

"Yes," says Maria, softly.

They sit together for a long time, content to share a promise.

It takes the men five days to cut the hay in the steaming
July sun. Their necks are burned, and their backs are sore.
But the hay is cut and dried and in the barn.

Meanwhile, Maria and her mother do their usual chores day after day, week after week: cleaning the cabin, making the meals, washing, mending, milking the cows, feeding the chickens, and baking the bread.

The baking oven is out in the yard, fired with branches of jack pine and red spruce. All the week's bread is made in one night and Maria stays up late, alone, moving the loaves around at the halfway point and waiting for them to be done. She has come to love these dark, quiet evenings, when she can think about François and dream of what their life together might be like. But there is so much time to wait until next spring! She imagines the joy of his return, bringing warmth and color to her drab gray world.

When the bread is ready, Maria finds it hard to interrupt her beautiful reverie.

$\mathcal{S}$oon it is September. The oats and wheat are yellow, dry from the summer drought, though not quite ready to harvest. This doesn't stop the cows, who manage to knock down a fence post or two every time they try to reach the golden feast.

October is coming. Rain and early frosts make the work slow and rob the grain of strength, but finally it is cut and stored in the barn – a small preparation for the mighty winter.

The first snow, though it quickly melts, is a warning. There is much
to be done before the deep cold sets in. The men plug holes in the
cabin and nail down anything that has come loose. On the inside,
the women stuff the cracks with rags and paste up old newspapers to
cover the drafts.

   The winter supply of firewood must be chopped, hauled, and piled
in the lean-to next to the cabin.

Winter has come. Some days the wind is so cold, it burns. The men do their chores with bent shoulders and faces hidden from the swirling snow.

"What a day to be in the forest!" says Maria, not realizing she has spoken out loud. She is thinking of François again.

Just before Christmas there is a heavy snowfall, blocking the road.

Samuel and Ti'Bé try to open a path with their shovels, but they come home without success, exhausted and shivering. There will be no chance of going to midnight mass on Christmas Eve. The snow reminds the family how far away they are from the villages, how isolated. . . .

Maria decides to say one thousand prayers that François Paradis will be safe in the forest and that spring will bring him back to her.

Christmas is celebrated quietly. Maria says her prayers and the children sing together while Samuel rocks Alma-Rose in the big chair.

Laura Chapdelaine hopes for company on New Year's Day, but no one comes. She cheers up the children by making maple syrup taffy on snow and they are chewing the first pieces when Eutrope Gagnon arrives.

"I have sad news," he says.

"Not my boys?" Maria's mother is alarmed.

"No, Madame. But someone else you care about." Eutrope glances at Maria. "It is François Paradis."

Maria's world falls silent, even as Eutrope explains.

"He told his boss he wanted to come up here for Christmas, but the trains weren't running because of an accident on the track."

He was coming to see me! Maria thinks.

"His heart was set," continues Eutrope. "He decided to walk. He must have missed the path in the storm. He lost his way. . . ."

No one can speak. They all know what the end must have been like for François.

"He was a good man," says Eutrope, quietly. "He was not to be matched."

$\mathcal{M}$aria has no words, though she knows the others are trying to comfort her. Together the family kneels to say a prayer for François.

Maria turns to the frost-covered window, but her eyes fill with tears and for a moment she cannot see.

She opens the door and steps out into the night. The slap of cold on her cheek makes her think of how François must have suffered. He was alone, probably hungry, exhausted, fighting the raging blizzard

and his growing fear. Maria says another prayer and shivers, imagining François stumbling and, finally, asleep in his bed of snow.

Maria knows she will not die of unhappiness, but she cannot just wash it away like mud from her boots.

On a Sunday in February, she rides with her father in the sleigh to mass in La Pipe. After the service, the priest speaks with Maria. He firmly tells her not to keep grieving for François, that she must put her sorrow behind her and think about the future.

In March, the Chapdelaines are invited to a party at the home of Ephrem Surprenant. Maria's mother is very excited to get out. The family crowd into the sleigh, hitch up Charles-Eugène, and drive eight miles through the woods to join the villagers of Honfleur.

Ephrem's nephew, Lorenzo, happily greets Maria. He is visiting again from the United States, and there are other guests recently arrived in Canada from France.

"We dreamt of a life in the great outdoors," the Frenchmen explain. "We didn't realize it would be so hard. And no one told us about the black flies!"

"Oh, it's hard in the beginning," says Laura Chapdelaine. "But there is no better life. You have no boss, you have your land and your animals, and you're free!"

"Free?" scoffs Lorenzo. "How can you be free if you have animals to look after? You are a slave to your animals and yet you can't live on a farm without them. You have to work from morning until night, month after month after month, with little rest, no pleasure, and a winter that lasts for seven months. In the city, no one would put up with such misery."

The wind howls around the house and the party continues. The men tell hunting tales and ghost stories, but Maria is only half-listening. Her thoughts have wandered to the dark secrets of the forest.

As they say good night, Lorenzo whispers to Maria that he will come to see her tomorrow.

Sure enough, the next morning brings sunshine and Lorenzo to Maria's doorstep. They go snowshoeing together, along the frozen banks of the Peribonka River. Lorenzo has more to add to last night's speech.

"You can't imagine," he says. "The city sidewalks are as flat as your table. There are electric lights and streetcars, theaters and circuses, and moving pictures at the cinema! There are more people in one place than you see in a year up here. I want you to come with me, Maria. I've never seen any girl like you. When I went home after my last visit, I got the shivers thinking you might become a farmer's wife and stay in this wretched place.

"You've always lived here," he continues. "You can't even dream about how it is somewhere else. But I love you and want you to be my wife. I want to astonish you with new sights. I want to make you happy."

Maria does not know how to reply. *Imagine living in a place where winter ends in March and leaves are green in April . . . where the streets are lit at night!*

"Think about what I've said, Maria. I'll come back and you can give me your answer then."

Someone must have mentioned to Eutrope Gagnon that Lorenzo had been to visit because the next Saturday Eutrope comes to call. He has always been careful and shy with Maria but now he speaks in a rush, as if he's afraid of missing his chance.

"I have always cared for you, Maria," he says. "I never spoke before because first I wanted my farm to be ready for us to live there together. And then I guessed that you liked François the best. But now I see this fellow from the United States trying to take you away, so I thought I'd better speak up."

Maria listens while Eutrope tells her his plan: he will clear the land and plant grain and build a house. With hard work, he will pay cash and stay out of debt. He hopes that Maria will marry him and keep house; that she will cook, milk the cows, clean the stable, work the fields, and live her life alone with him in the woods.

Maria feels *no!* She does not want to live that way. But she cannot tell him yet. "Eutrope, I'm not ready to answer. You will have to wait."

She realizes he is disappointed as he goes away, but she needs time to think. Since she loves neither Lorenzo nor Eutrope the way she loved François, she must look at the other parts of the choice. She knows that her parents would want her to marry Eutrope. He lives nearby and they understand his ways. Lorenzo is offering an adventure far from home, away from the bleak and hostile forest where François died. Perhaps life in a far-off place could fill the longing that François has left behind.

Although she does not yet say it aloud, Maria has decided to marry Lorenzo.

One evening in April, Maria's mother does not want her supper. "I don't feel well," she says. "My body is sore and I'm tired. You make the bread tonight, Maria. I'm going to lie down."

No one is too concerned. It is a hard life; occasional aches and pains are part of it. But after three days, the family begins to get anxious.

"I'm burning up!" moans Laura Chapdelaine. "I'm going to die!"

"*Tsk*," says her husband. "Heaven is already full of old women. But we have only one here and you can still be useful from time to time."

He is worried enough, though, to accept Eutrope's offer of pills, even without knowing what they're for. Maria brings her mother water several times through the night, but when Laura is worse the next day, Samuel hitches up the sleigh to fetch the doctor from a distant town.

Maria counts the hours until finally, after a whole day of listening to her mother suffer, she hears the sleigh bells approach. The doctor examines Laura, but has not seen illness like this before. He has no cure. He borrows Charles-Eugène, saying he will return the next day. But Laura knows she is dying and tears roll down her face.

When Eutrope Gagnon arrives, he suggests that perhaps the bone-setter from Saint-Félicien would come to see the patient. He is thought to have ways of curing people for whom others have lost hope.

"But the doctor has the horse," says Maria. "How can we go thirty-five miles to Saint-Félicien?"

"I will walk," says Eutrope. "I will walk the eight miles to Honfleur and borrow a horse and sleigh from there." He sets off running, spurred on by Maria's grateful look.

A long day ticks by, marked by visits from the priest and the doctor once again. The priest hears Laura's confession and gives her absolution.

Eutrope returns with the bonesetter in the middle of the night, who gently examines the sick woman. Sadly he, too, is unable to

help. Despite the rising blizzard outside, he urges the family to bring the priest back to Laura's bedside so that she may be comforted before she dies.

The priest arrives in time. He brushes snow from his coat and hurries to bring peace to the patient and the rest of the Chapdelaines. The howling wind stops just as Laura takes her last sighing breath.

"Your mother was a good woman, Maria," says Samuel. "She was brave and wise. There was none like her."

"I know, Papa, I know."

Samuel tells stories about his married life with Laura, about the different farms where they worked so hard to claim the land, and about the time she scared a bear away from the sheep by chasing it with a stick.

"Maybe I shouldn't have made her move so much and live so far in the bush. Maybe we should have stayed in a village, where she could have been close to the church and her neighbors."

Maria sees that her father is full of regret and grief. She wonders whether her mother would think the life of hardship had been worth it. She knows there are not many women who have the strength or courage to live such a life. A life of toil and discomfort. A life of difficulty and loneliness. Maria knows she does not want such a life for herself.

And yet . . .

If she goes with Lorenzo to the great shiny city, will she be happy? Will the streets and the stores and the easy life make her content? What will she do on an early spring morning if she does not see the first tiny buds pushing their way toward the sun? What will it be like on a hot summer evening if she can't step outside to feel a cool breeze scented with the forest?

Rain patters on the roof of the cabin. Maria thinks about little Alma-Rose, who will need her now that their mother is gone. *It seems I will be staying here,* she realizes.

When Eutrope asks her again, in May, if she has made her decision, Maria answers with all her heart. "Yes, next spring at seeding time, I'll marry you." The quiet of the forest settles around Maria and she is at peace.